M.P. ROBERTSON studied illustration at Kingston University. He is an internationally acclaimed author and illustrator of children's books. His many books for Frances Lincoln include *The Egg*, *The Dragon Snatcher*, *Frank 'n' Stan*, *Food Chain*, *Hieronymus Betts and His Unusual Pets* and *Ice Trap!*, written by Meredith Hooper. He lives with his family in Wiltshire. When he isn't writing and illustrating, he enjoys visiting schools to share his love of drawing and stories. To find out more about Mark's books or to book a visit, please go to **www.mprobertson.com**

Text and illustrations copyright © Mark Robertson 2002, 2014

The right of M.P. Robertson to be identified as the author and illustrator of this Work has been asserted by him in accordance with the Copyright, Designs and Patent Act, 1988.

First published in Great Britain in 2002.

This early reader edition first published in Great Britain and in the USA in 2014 by Frances Lincoln Children's Books, 74-77 White Lion Street, London N1 9PF

www.franceslincoln.com

A CIP catalogue record for this book is available from the British Library.

978-1-84780-552-2

Printed in China

1 3 5 7 9 8 6 4 2

The Great
DRAGON RESCUE

M.P. Robertson

F

FRANCES LINCOLN
CHILDREN'S BOOKS

George was bored. When it came to fighting, chickens were not as brave as dragons. One morning, as George was collecting eggs and daydreaming about dragonish things, he felt the chicken coop shudder.

When he looked out, he knew an adventure
had begun.

Up, up they soared, George, the dragon and the chicken coop.

They flew faster and faster until they came to a land where everything began with Once upon a time.

They landed in a dark forest. The dragon led George through the trees until they could see a flickering light ahead.

From behind a tree they watched a witch cook toads
on a dragon's flame. The dragon was only a chick,
just out of the egg. It looked very sad.

George and the dragon waited until the witch had gobbled her way through a cauldron full of toads. Soon they could hear her snores rattling the windows of the cottage.

George struggled to open the cage. The witch's crow flapped around the cage croaking, "Wake up – wake up, witch! Someone is stealing the dragon!"

The witch came bursting out, her wand crackling
with spells.
"Who dares to steal my dragon?" she roared.
George had read enough fairy tales to know that
witches are very boastful. "I don't believe you are a
witch," he said. "Real witches can fly on broomsticks."
"I am a real witch! I am the quickest, wickedest witch
in the west," she bragged.

"My dragon has beaten the wicked witches
of the north, south and east," George fibbed.
"I bet he can beat you too!"
"I bet he couldn't," sneered the witch. "Let's race
around the enchanted castle and back. When I win,
I'll turn you both into toads for my tea." She jumped
on her broomstick, "On your marks. Get set . . ."
And she was gone.

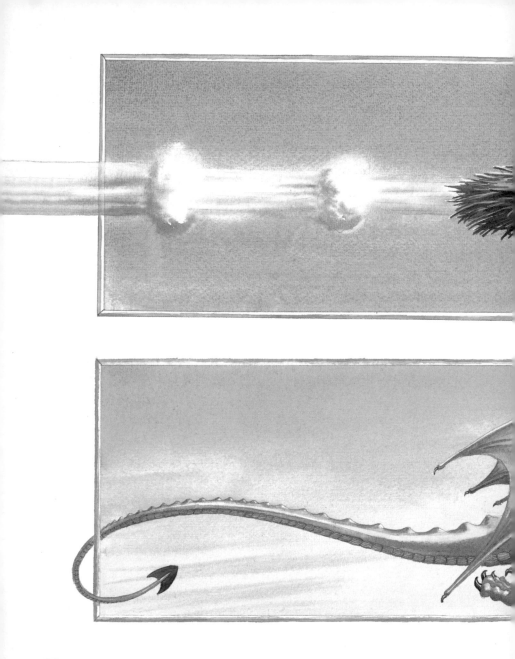

The witch was frighteningly fast . . .

but the dragon was faster.

Soon the witch and the dragon were neck and neck.

As the enchanted castle came into view, the dragon was in the lead.

George looked back to see the witch weaving
a spell.

But George had a secret weapon. Just before the spell was cast, he pelted the witch with eggs.

The witch was in a terrible rage. There was a
blinding flash – but the egg that dripped from
her wand had scrambled the spell.

By the time they landed on the witch's roof, all that was left of the witch was her broomstick and her hat. George lifted the hat, carefully.

There was a fat ugly toad hidden under it. "It will be a hundred years before a prince kisses that!" he thought.

George set the baby dragon free. It ran to the big
dragon with a roar of delight.

George didn't speak Dragon, but he knew exactly what the baby had said . . . . "Daddy."

It was time for George to return home. The chickens would be missing their coop.

Up, up they soared, and George waved goodbye to the
land where everything ended with Happily ever after.
But not if you are a witch . . . or a toad!

Collect the TIME TO READ books:

978-1-84780-476-1

978-1-84780-475-4

978-1-84780-477-8

978-1-84780-478-5

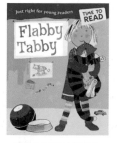

978-1-84780-543-0

978-1-84780-544-7

978-1-84780-542-3

978-1-84780-545-4

978-1-84780-549-2

978-1-84780-551-5

978-1-84780-552-2

978-1-84780-550-8